The STAR WARS™

BOOK of

Monsters, Ooze, and Slime

The STAR WARS™ Book of

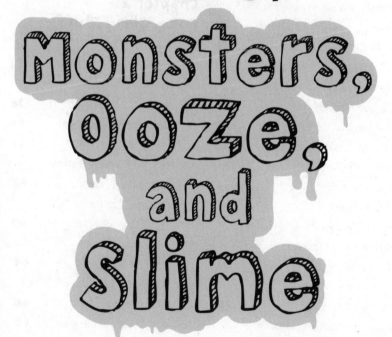

Monsters, Ooze, and Slime

written and illustrated
by Katie Cook

Contents

CHAPTER 3:
Creepy Critters

CHAPTER 4:
Monster Madness

Glossary

Introduction

welcome, brave traveler!

The **galaxy** is an amazing place,
but are you **sure** you know what
you're in for? Have you ever heard
of Geonosian **brain worms**
or slimy, ravenous **rathtars?**

Are you **really sure** that you
want to go exploring?

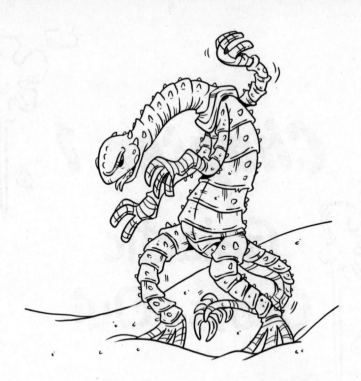

If so, you'd better **be prepared!**

Do you want to know who has the **biggest teeth?** Which bug has the most **poisonous** sting? Which monster is **so big** it could swallow you and your whole house in **one gulp?**

Read on, and learn the **grossest, scariest,** most **disgusting** facts from across the stars!

Chapter 1

Galactic Gross-Out

A complete guide to all the questions you don't want answered.

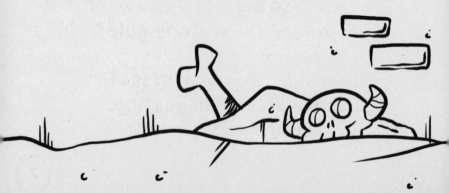

What is the *smelliest* thing in the galaxy?

There are a **lot** of options:

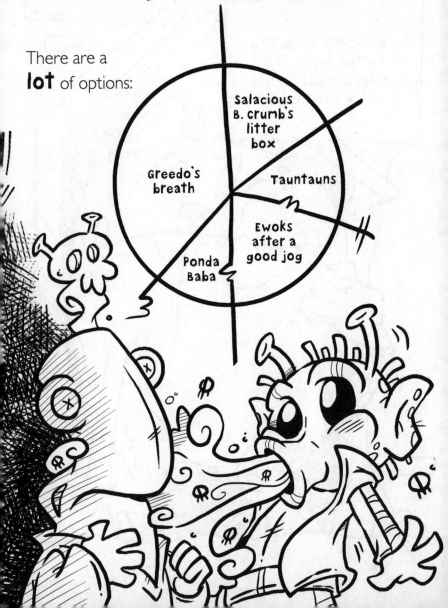

Salacious B. Crumb's litter box

Greedo's breath

Tauntauns

Ewoks after a good jog

Ponda Baba

So what *does* a tauntaun smell like?

Tauntaun odor should have its own chapter. **Really.**
Their hides give off a smell like **moldy cheese.**

But on the inside? **Rotting dragonsnake eggs** combined with **rancor mucus** that's been left out in the sun.

Where is the worst place in the galaxy to live?

There are many contenders, but one stands out: **Kessel.**

Not only will you have to follow a super-dangerous path to get there, once you arrive it'll be less than enjoyable.

The hot **spice mines** are full of **cruel guards, angry droids,** and **misery.**

Go somewhere else for your vacation.

We would recommend Alderaan, a lovely place to…

…Oh. Never mind.

It has been (0) days since our last droid uprising!

Can Ewoks get *fleas?*

CLOSE-UP

Well, the tiny **termidote** on the Forest Moon of Endor is similar to what we call a flea. It bites furry creatures and causes **SO MUCH ITCHING.**

The termidote does **this** to an Ewok:

SCRATCH!

Do Ewoks really *eat* people?

They'll eat pretty much anything… as Wicket's mother always said, "If you don't **try it,** how do you know you **don't like it?**"

Why does General Grievous cough ?

Some people say he's still getting used to his metal **cyborg body.**

Others say his cowardly ways produce a **nervous tic.** However, it could just be that he has the dreaded curse of seasonal **allergies!**

What is in that bag on his *chest?*

It's his **vital organs!**

They are some of the few non-metal parts left of him. **Gross!**

Which species has the most eyes?

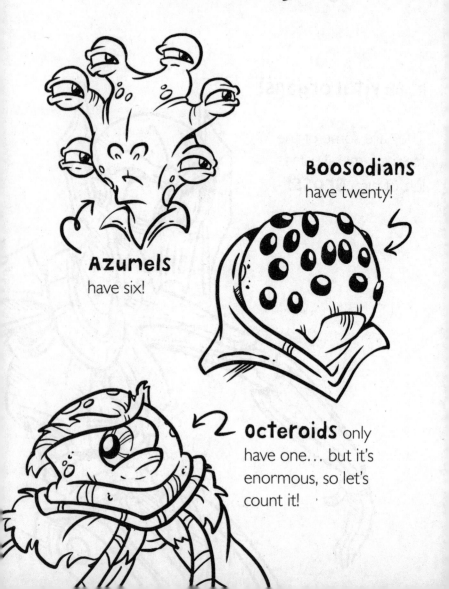

Boosodians
have twenty!

Azumels
have six!

Octeroids only
have one… but it's
enormous, so let's
count it!

Do some species have more than one brain?

- Brain 1

- Brain 2

Ki-Adi-Mundi
Occupation: Jedi
Species: Cerean
Number of brains:
Two (very smart!)

Fode and Beed
Occupation:
Podrace announcers
Species: Troig
Number of brains:
Two (not as smart)

What do people eat on *Tatooine?*

They mostly eat **dried plants** and **seeds,** but crispy **fried bugs** are also a local delicacy!

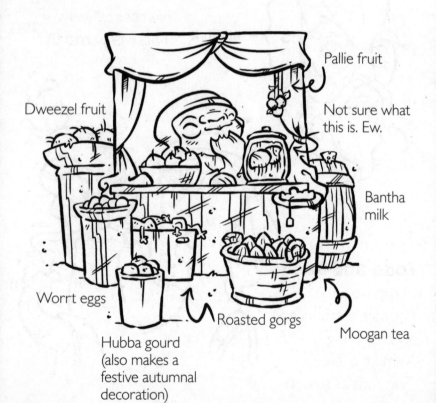

Pallie fruit

Dweezel fruit

Not sure what this is. Ew.

Bantha milk

Worrt eggs

Roasted gorgs

Moogan tea

Hubba gourd (also makes a festive autumnal decoration)

Why are *Tusken Raiders* covered in bandages?

Some say **Tusken Raiders** use the bandages
to protect their skin from the burning Tatooine sun…
Others say it's to keep them from being overpowered
by the **smell of the banthas** they ride.

Why do some people not have heads?

Creepy **Doctor Evazan** is known throughout the galaxy for his… experiments.

One of his experiments involves removing people's **brains** so they can be controlled!

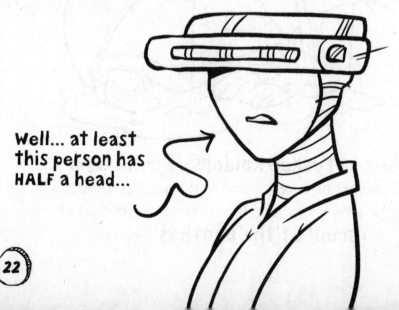

Well... at least this person has HALF a head...

What is the muckiest planet in the galaxy ❓

It's **Mimban.**

Mud, mud, mud. **Everywhere.**

Mud in your shoes, mud in your hair, mud in your pockets.

SPLORT

Yet another place to **avoid** on your vacation…

If the **muck** and **angry locals** don't keep you from visiting, maybe the Imperial **stormtroopers** will?

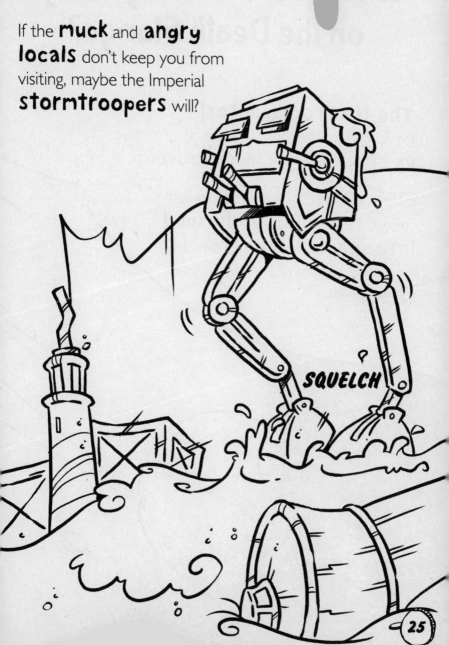

SQUELCH

Where does all the garbage on the Death Star go?

The trash compactor!

It's a big machine that squashes all of the garbage so that it takes up less room.

Before the Death Star jumps to light speed, the garbage is just **dumped into space,** leaving it to become a garbage asteroid for other ships to dodge. Ew.

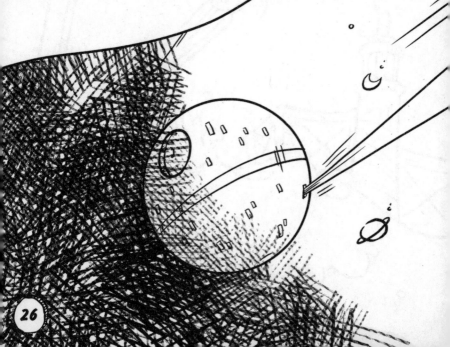

What would happen if you fell off of Cloud City?

How do different species eat?

Ithorians (Momaw Nadon)

Your guess is as good as any.

Possible relative?

Mon calamari (Admiral Ackbar)

ACKBAR! NO!

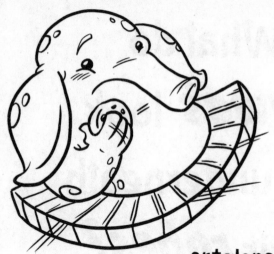

Ortolans (Max Rebo)
Ortolans have no mouth, so they absorb their food through suckers on their toes. Tasty!

Dugs (Sebulba)
Well, those are probably cleaner than this hands.

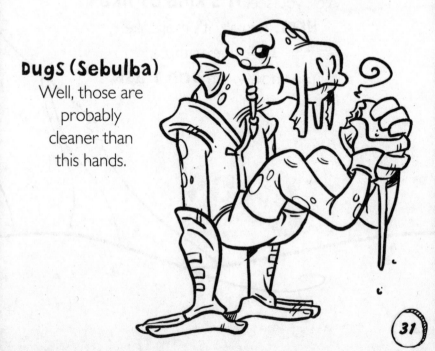

What do **Jawas** look like underneath their **robes?**

Well, you see, **it's kind of like**…
Hrm. Actually it's more like…
Err, there's this…
You know what? **Don't ask.**

Eww!

Chapter 2

Oozy, Slimy Stuff

GOO, goop, ick, muck, snot, and more!

Does
Jabba the Hutt
ever take a bath ?

Not very often, but yes!
His **servants lower him**
into his bath and scrub the rough Tatooine
sand from his... **well, everything.**

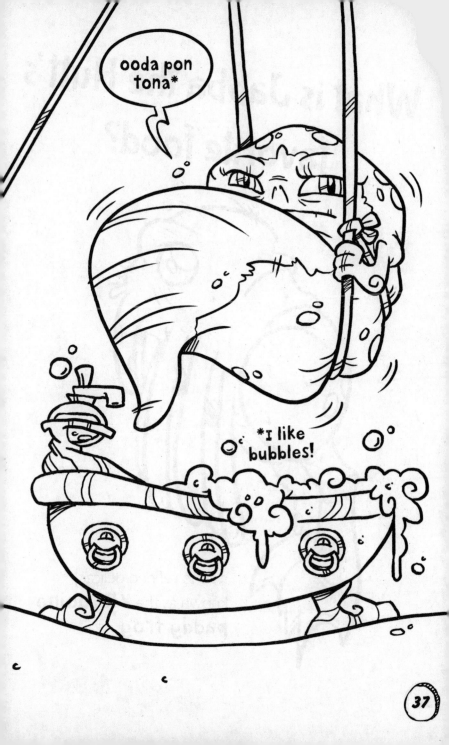

What is Jabba the Hutt's favorite food?

Eww!

It's the refined delicacy known as the **Klatooine paddy frog.**

Groosss!

Tempted? Jabba eats them **alive** and **raw,** but if you don't want to deal with the shrill **screaming** as it wiggles down your throat, try roasting yours in a butter sauce with a side of hubba gourd.

Or try a hearty **paddy frog stew?**

What does *blue milk* taste like?

Did you know it comes from **banthas?**
Even though banthas smell terrible, their milk is
actually **very tasty.** It has hints of coconut!

What about the *green milk?*

You'll have to ask
Luke Skywalker about
the **green milk...**

In all the galaxy, which creature makes the *worst slime* ?

Well, the **rancor** produces a stinky, **slimy drool** that will cover you in a sticky coating before he eats you. But the tiny **voorpak** is also a contender for… reasons you don't want to know.

Which creature has the strongest tongue?

The humble **frog-dog** can pull almost **120 kilograms** (265 pounds) with just its tongue!

And LOOK AT ITS **CUTE WIDDLE FACE!**

What's the *slimiest thing* in the galaxy?

It's **Jabba the Hutt!**
Not only is his big, **slug-like body**
covered in slime, but he **acts** awfully slimy too!

45

What, actually, is *bantha poodoo*?

Despite how it sounds, it's actually **bantha food!**

…it still **smells terrible** though.

Are there **zombies** in the galaxy?

Well, there is the **Geonosian brain worm...**
It can infect a host and take over its brain and motor
functions... even if that host is dead. **GAHHHHHH!**

Is the *Emperor* a zombie?

Nope! He used the power of the **Sith** to send his mind into a **cloned body** made by his followers. **Handy!**

Chapter 3

Creepy Critters

**The worst pets
in the galaxy...
and other facts.**

Do some people really *eat* bugs?

Of course! Many species do. Make sure you eat the thorax—there's so much protein!

Gungans

Trandoshans

Chadra-Fan

Anzellans

Which bug has the worst *sting*?

Oof. That's going to be the **kouhun**.
One jab and you're down for good!

What are some of the _strangest_ species?

Duracrete Slug
Eats rocks! Where's the fun in that?

Dianoga
Lives in garbage. Thrilled to do so.

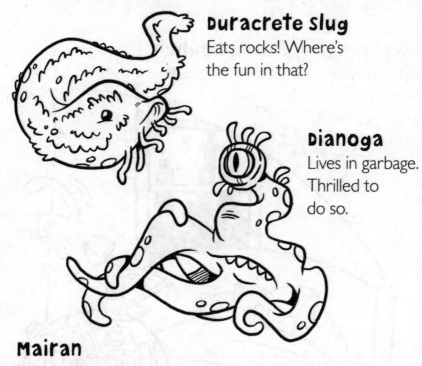

Mairan
Inadvisable to let one hug you. They can read your mind!

What's the *biggest* bug?

The majestic **gelagrub** from the forests
of Felucia. So graceful. **So squishy.**

What's the most *poisonous* creature?

There are **so many** poisonous creatures in the galaxy, but one that really strikes fear into people is the **Tatooine rock wart.** This little parasite can take out a ronto!

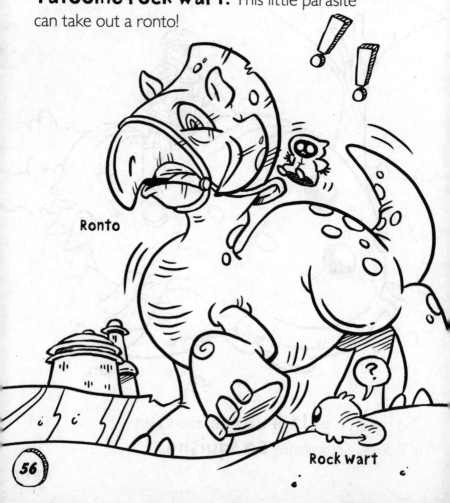

Ronto

Rock wart

What's the **creepiest** creepy-crawly ?

The **krykna.** Imagine a big, **spider-like creature** that's resistant to blasters and reacts to your negative, terrified emotions? Uh... **no thank you.**

Are Geonosians really giant bugs ?

If it **flies** like a bug and **sounds** like a bug…

And **builds homes** like a bug…

And **looks** like a bug…

Well… it's probably a bug.

But you shouldn't call them out on it unless you're prepared to be fed to giant beasts in their arena.

59

Chapter 4

Monster Madness

The worst of the worst, or the best of the best? You decide!

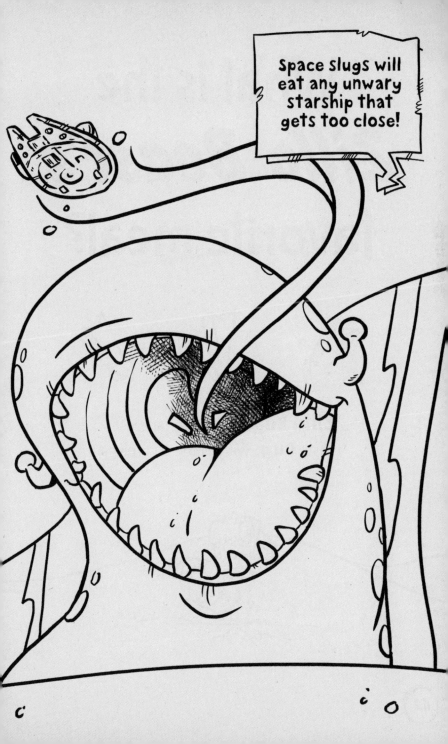

What is the Zillo Beast's favorite meal?

The **Zillo Beast** of Malastare just loves
a tasty **Dug,** with all the trimmings.

What's in the
Sarlacc's belly?

All those creatures that Jabba has fed to it. Hopefully someone has a **deck of sabacc cards** to play with as they're slowly digested over **1,000 years.**

Seriously though, getting eaten by the Sarlacc must be one of the **worst things** that can happen to you. It must be **hot, dark,** and **very icky** in there!

What's the biggest monster in the galaxy?

The **Summa-verminoth!** Hopefully you aren't planning to make the **Kessel Run** anytime soon, because this **gigantic** monster lurks nearby!

Length:
**7,500 meters
(24,600 feet)**

What's the biggest thing that it could eat?

Well, it's very fond
of **starships...**
and what's inside them.

What do rancors eat?

Pretty much anything… they are **not picky.**
They are quite fond of chewing on pig-like
Gamorreans, though.

What monster has the *biggest* teeth?

An **exogorth!** Known commonly as a space slug,
this giant species can crush a space cruiser in one bite!

What's the deadliest creature?

Listen, there is a very long list of creatures in the galaxy that will happily chase you down and eat you. **Wampas, rancors, space Slugs, nexu...**

But worst of all, never cross a **porg.**
Just kidding. But don't let them near your lightsaber.
Accidents can happen.

What's lurking in the *swampy* depths of Dagobah?

If you see a swirling tail under the water, it's most likely a ferocious **dragonsnake.** It's probably best if you don't go for a swim!

What's the biggest thing in the waters of Naboo ?

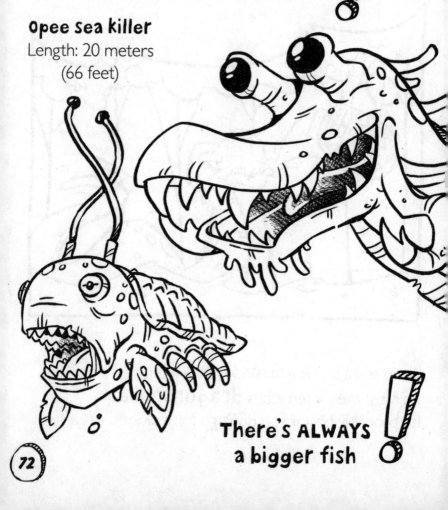

Opee sea killer
Length: 20 meters
(66 feet)

There's ALWAYS a bigger fish

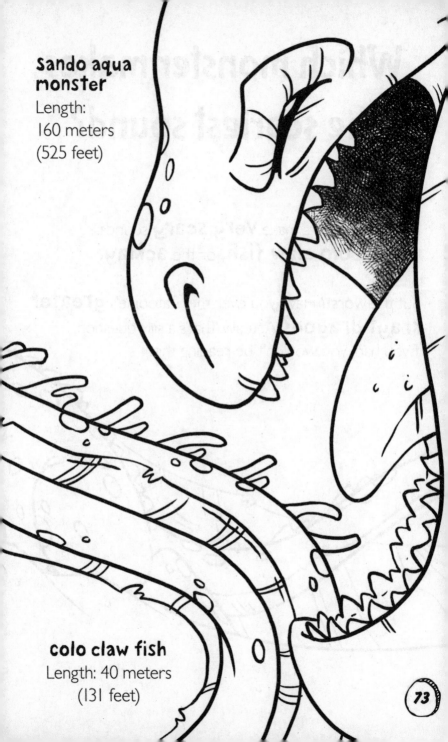

sando aqua monster
Length:
160 meters
(525 feet)

colo claw fish
Length: 40 meters
(131 feet)

Which monster makes the scariest sound?

Lots of monsters make **very scary** sounds.
Like the **colo claw fish,** or the **acklay.**

But the worst? Have you ever met Tatooine's **greater krayt dragon?** Actually, that's a silly question…
if you had, you wouldn't be reading this.

Which predator has the best sense of smell?

If a **corellian hound** is ever told to hunt you down… well, let's hope you can run fast.

Which predator has the best eyesight?

Some argue the tiny Pasaana **oki-poki** does, but perhaps it's the terrifying Anaxes **fyrnock.** If you come across a fyrnock at night, it's already too late.

What is that *monster* in the trash compactor on the *Death Star?*

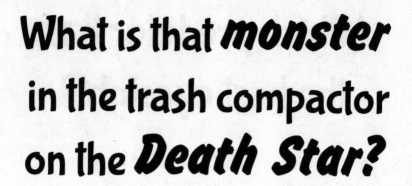

It's a **dianoga,** and there is more to it than meets the eye… Under the surface of all that gross brown water is a **tentacled beast** ready to pull you under!

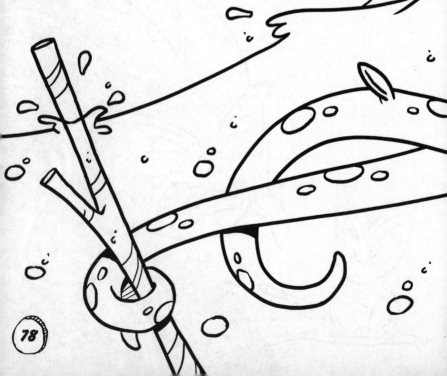

Are there any *friendly* monsters?

Just because a creature is **big,** or **weird-looking,** that doesn't make it a **monster!** How could you call the chunky **happabore** a monster! Or the gentle **fambaa?** Or the sweet **kaadu?** How dare you!

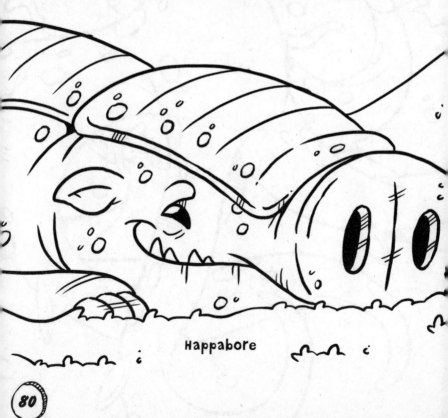

Happabore

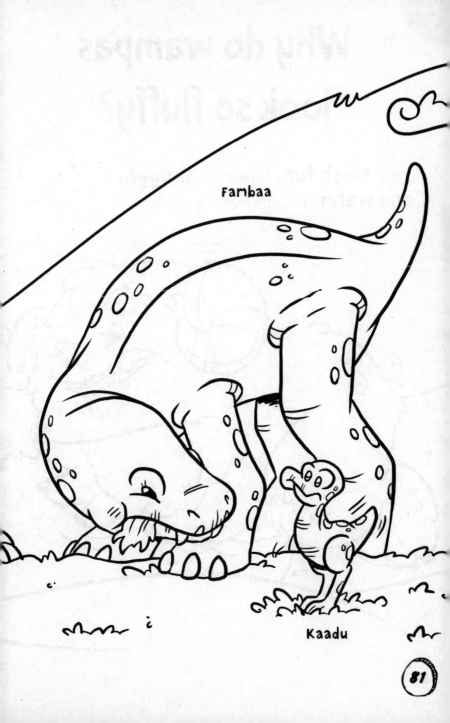

Fambaa

Kaadu

Why do wampas look so fluffy?

Their **thick fur** keeps them **snuggly and warm** in Hoth's freezing snow.

Also, it acts as **camouflage,**
so this **ravenous predator**
can sneak up on its prey…

What do *wampas* do with their prey?

Well, they don't have a **conversation** with it... They **stick it in the ice** to keep it **fresh** before they munch on it!

What's the scariest
monster?

First on the list would be a **rathtar**.
Second on that list is also a **rathtar**.
It is also **third** on that list.

Why is everyone so *scared* of rathtars?

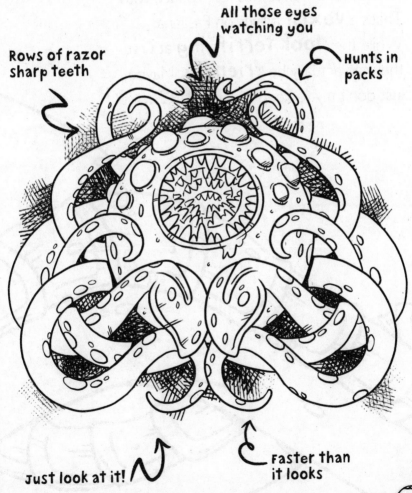

Rows of razor sharp teeth

All those eyes watching you

Hunts in packs

Just look at it!

Faster than it looks

What is that giant snake thing?

Oh, the one Rey comes face to face with? That's a **vexis!** It lives on Pasaana. While they **look terrifying** at first, they can actually be **friendly**. Maybe just don't try to keep one as a **pet...**

What is the *deadliest* arena beast on *Geonosis* ❓

All of them. The answer is **all of them.**

Nexu

Reek

Acklay

Are there any *monsters* out in space?

Yes, and they come in all shapes and sizes!

Giant **purgill** are very much misunderstood! They are **gentle** and enjoy floating next to starships. But sometimes they just get a little **too close...**

On the other hand, **mynocks** are just waiting in the wings to tear your ship apart! **Avoid** at all costs!

Glossary

Allergies when something causes your body to react badly, for example by sneezing or swelling up

Camouflage something that helps a person, creature, or object stay hidden

Candidate a possible choice for a particular job or role

Convenient easy to use

Cyborg something that is part alive, part machine

Delicacy a tasty food that is particularly popular in a specific place

Ferocious savage and fierce

Gigantic really large

Inadvisable when something is a bad idea

Kessel Run the route that starships traveling to the planet Kessel must follow. It passes through the dangerous Akkadese Maelstrom

Misunderstood when something is believed to be a certain way, but is actually a different way

Occupation someone's job

Pressure the force of something squeezing inward or pushing outward

Ravenous extremely hungry

Sabacc a card game that is very popular in the *Star Wars* galaxy

Terrifying very scary

Thorax the middle part of a creature's body. In insects, it's where the legs and wings attach

Trimmings the extras that you have with a meal

Unwary when someone isn't paying attention to what is happening around them

Uprising an event when people who are controlled fight back against those who control them

Vital organs parts of your body that are needed to keep you alive, such as heart, lungs, and liver

Senior Editor David Fentiman
Project Art Editor Stefan Georgiou
Senior Production Editor Jennifer Murray
Senior Production Controller Louise Minihane
Managing Editor Sarah Harland
Managing Art Editor Vicky Short
Publishing Director Mark Searle

First American Edition, 2021
Published in the United States by
DK Publishing
1450 Broadway, Suite 801,
New York, NY 10018

Page design copyright © 2021
Dorling Kindersley Limited
DK, a Division of
Penguin Random House LLC
21 22 23 24 25 10 9 8 7 6 5 4 3 2 1
001–321734–Apr/2021

© & TM 2021 Lucasfilm Ltd.

A catalog record for this book
is available from the Library of
Congress.

ISBN 978-0-7440-2730-3
(Paperback)
ISBN 978-0-7440-3127-0
(Hardcover)

DK books are available at special
discounts when purchased
in bulk for sales promotions,
premiums, fund-raising, or
educational use. For details,
contact:
DK Publishing Special Markets,
1450 Broadway, Suite 801,
New York, NY 10018
SpecialSales@dk.com

Printed in China

For the curious

www.dk.com

MIX
Paper from
responsible sources
FSC™ C018179

This book is made from
Forest Stewardship Council™
certified paper—one small
step in DK's commitment
to a sustainable future.